My Pencil and Me

and Me

by Sara Varon

What's the big deal?
Can't you just find another pencil?
No, this is a really special pencil. If it weren't for this very pencil, you wouldn't even be in this story.
Wow. Deep.

thanks to Ellen Lindner for the baseball inspiration,
and to the Pigeons for being a great flock of teammates.

:01

First Second

Copyright © 2020 by Sara Varon

Published by First Second
First Second is an imprint of Roaring Brook Press, a division of Holtzbrinck Publishing Holdings Limited Partnership
120 Broadway, New York, NY 10271

Don't miss your next favorite book from First Second!
For the latest updates go to Firstsecondnewsletter.com and sign up for our enewsletter.

All rights reserved
Library of Congress Control Number: 2019948144

ISBN: 978-1-59643-589-6

Our books may be purchased in bulk for promotional, educational, or business use.
Please contact your local bookseller or the Macmillan Corporate and Premium Sales
Department at (800) 221-7945 ext. 5442 or by email at MacmillanSpecialMarkets@macmillan.com.

FIRST
EDITION

First edition, 2020

Edited by Mark Siegel and Kiara Valdez
Cover design by Andrew Arnold
Interior design by Kirk Benshoff
Printed in China by RR Donnelley Asia Printing Solutions Ltd., Dongguan City, Guangdong Province

Photo of the bookstore in the interior, shot by Matt Carr, is Stories Bookshop + Storytelling Lab in Brooklyn, New York
Endpaper photo shot by Aaron Meshon

Sketched in pencil on plain old photocopy paper with a Koh-I-Noor Rapidomatic 0.9 mm
mechanical pencil and 2B lead. Final art inked with a Pentel Pocket brush pen on
Strathmore Bristol paper with vellum surface. Colored digitally in Photoshop.

1 3 5 7 9 10 8 6 4 2

BY ART
WE LIVE

Written by
Steve Tiller

Illustrated by
Robert Cremeans

To Beau —
The Santa
Fly The Express!
Merry Christmas —
Steve Tiller

MICHAELSMIND

Steve Tiller, Author
Robert Cremeans, Illustrator / Creative Director
Kathryn L. Tecosky, Editor
Mary Huggins, Grammarian

Special thanks to: Our Families, The Hudgens Center for the Arts, CCAD, David & Melissa Abbey, Brian Bias our Apple guru.

Library of Congress Cataloging-in-Publication Data
Tiller, Steve

Summary:
Santa meets an alien and heads to the stars taking the true message of Christmas, and a few presents to the universe and beyond.

ISBN 0-9704597-9-3
[1. Christmas - Children's Fiction.   2. Santa Claus - Fiction.   3. Christian - Faith]

Printed by
Regal Printing Hong Kong

Illustrations in this book were created on a Macintosh G4 computer using Adobe Photoshop and a mouse!

Visit us for fun and games at:
www.michaelsmind.com